Gift
from
Robert N. Mimin

LITTLE OWL

AN EIGHTFOLD BUDDHIST ADMONITION

Janwillem van de Wetering ▪ Illustrated by Marc Brown

Houghton Mifflin Company Boston 1978

Library of Congress Cataloging in Publication Data

Wetering, Janwillem van de, 1931-
    Little Owl.

    SUMMARY: Uses animal characters to present an inter-
pretation of the Eight Buddhist Admonitions.
    1. Eightfold Path—Juvenile literature. [1. Eight-
fold Path. 2. Buddhism] I. Brown, Marc Tolon.
II. Title
BQ4320.W47   294.3'4'44   77-27452
ISBN 0-395-26456-1

H 10 9 8 7 6 5 4 3 2 1

Preface

When the Indian prince Siddharta, some
two thousand five hundred years ago,
became a Buddha (which is Sanskrit and means
'he who knows') he founded a religion
that is called Buddhism, one of the major
religions of this planet with many many
millions of followers.

Buddha recommended a method that, he claimed,
would lead to supreme insight or enlightenment.
The method is known as the Buddhist Eightfold
Path and its aspects are Right Insight,
Right Intentions, Right Talking, Right Action,
Right Livelihood, Right Effort, Right Awareness,
and Right Meditation.

The concept is that we should
try and keep all aspects in mind while we live
but sometimes this isn't done and one aspect
becomes much more important that the others.

In this book Little Owl prattles so much
about insight that he irritates the other
animals and comes to grief, Little Koala
spends his time chanting about love, Kitten
tries to do right but isn't aware of his
situation, Little Squirrel gets a little too
involved with making his daily nut, Little Rhino
blunders into an immovalble object, Little Rabbit
has a nervous breakdown while he watches what
isn't there and Little Sloth almost cripples himself
while concentrating on the emptiness of the sky.

But all troubles are temporary and when the
little animals meet and decide to try *together*
a marvellous journey begins.

Chapter One

ONCE
upon a time
not so very long ago
Little Owl was listening to his mother. He didn't really feel like listening to her, because he had other things to do, but he was a reasonably polite little owl, so he listened.

"Little Owl," Mother Owl said.
"Yes, mother," Little Owl said.
"Listen to me."
"Yes, mother,"
"Little Owl," Mother Owl asked, "do you know what's most important in life?"

Little Owl thought for a while.
His mother looked very serious, peering at him with her big round eyes.

"Right wisdom," Little Owl squeaked.

"Yes," his mother said, lifting a wing and flapping it about. "RIGHT WISDOM. Very good. We owls are wise, we know great truths."

"Yes," Little Owl said in his most convincing manner.

His mother moved a little closer and bent down so that she could whisper into Little Owl's ear.

"We owls," she whispered, "don't only learn HOW to do things, we also find out WHY we do them."

"Why?" Little Owl squeaked.

"Yes," Mother Owl said and nodded. "Why!"

Little Owl ran off. He flew a bit as well, and he kept on talking to himself. "Why," he said. "We owls find out why we do things. We owls are wise. We think a lot. We think out real answers. And then we tell all the other animals about the real answers, so that they can become wise, too — just like us owls."

Little Owl looked down. He saw a wild boar. The wild boar was

standing in a clearing in the forest below him. Little Owl flew
down and sat on the ground, right in front of the wild boar.

The wild boar looked up. "Go away," the wild boar said in a
deep voice.

"What are you doing?" Little Owl asked.

"Looking for grubs," the wild boar said. "Now go away. You're
bothering me."

"Do you know how to look for grubs?" Little Owl asked.

"Of course," the wild boar said. "I've been doing it all my life. I just dig about with my snout, like this. But why am I talking to you? Go away."

"Do you know WHY you are looking for grubs?" Little Owl asked.

The wild boar sighed impatiently. "Yes," he said, "because I am hungry. GO AWAY!"

"No," said Little Owl. "I must tell you something very important. Something you don't know about yet. But I do because I am an owl."

"Yes?" the wild boar asked slowly and showed its great yellow fangs.

"Yes," Little Owl said confidently, and he hopped up and down. "You are looking for grubs because you want to go on living, you see. You want to feed yourself. That's very good. You will live longer. And the longer you live the more chances you will have to find real answers — about your life, you see? About *why* you are alive and . . ."

But Little Owl could say no more. The boar took a deep breath and charged. And Little Owl was left lying flat on his back.

When his mother found him, Little Owl was still on his back.
His wing was sore and he was crying. She took him home
and put him to bed.

"Mother," Little Owl said after he had stayed in bed for some
time.

"Yes, dear?"

"I am bored. Will I have to stay in bed much longer?"

"Another few days, dear."

"Ah," Little Owl said in a sad voice.

"Don't fret, dear. I'll tell you a story."

Chapter Two

_____

ONCE
upon a time
not so very long ago
Little Koala Bear was listening to his mother. He didn't really
feel like listening to her, because he had other things to do,
but he was a reasonably polite little koala bear, so he listened.

"Little Koala Bear," Mother Koala Bear said.
"Yes, mother," Little Koala Bear said.
"Listen to me."
"Yes, mother."
"Little Koala Bear," Mother Koala Bear asked, "do you know
what's most important in life?"

Little Koala Bear thought for a long time. He wasn't very good
at thinking. His mother was looking at him, and he
kept on trying to think, and his furry little face got smaller
and smaller, and his ears stood up, and he had three
deep wrinkles in his forehead. And he thought and thought.
"Well?" Mother Koala Bear asked.
"The most important thing in life is to mean well," Little Koala
Bear answered.

"Good." his mother said. "RIGHT INTENTIONS, that's all that matters — to mean well, to love all the other animals, and to be good to them. Just remember that."

RIGHT INTENTIONS

His mother climbed higher into the eucalyptus tree, and Little Koala Bear moved up the branch and began to munch leaves. The sun shone, and the clouds drifted along above him, and he could hear the big waves from the sea splashing on the beach behind the forest.

"I mean well, I mean well," Little Koala Bear sang to himself as he ate. He looked down at the kangaroos who were jumping around below his tree looking for grass, and he looked up at the kookaburras who flew above him and cackled HAW HAW HAW, and he said to them, "I love you all."

But they weren't listening. So, to get their attention, he began to sing very loud.

"LOVE, LOVE, LOVE," sang Little Koala Bear.

But they still weren't listening. So he stood up on his branch, and he waved at them with both paws, and he sang, "LOVE,"

and fell all the way down to the ground.

BAM!

"Oh dear," Mother Koala Bear said, and she climbed down.
"Oh dear," Father Koala Bear said, and he climbed down, too.
They carried him up into the tree and asked him how he
was, but all Little Koala Bear could do was point at his head
and cry.

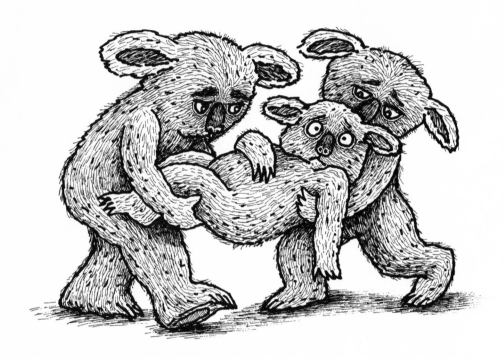

Mother Koala Bear made him a nice soft nest out of
eucalyptus leaves and put him into it.

After a few days his head didn't hurt so much any more. He
wanted to play with the other little koala bears, but his
mother shook her head.

"No dear."

"Please, mother," Little Koala Bear begged.

"No, you'll have to stay here for a few more days, dear," Mother
Koala Bear said, "but I'll tell you a story."

Chapter Three

ONCE
upon a time
not so very long ago
Little Crow was listening to his mother. He didn't really feel
like listening to her, because he had other things to do, but he
was a reasonably polite little crow, so he listened.

"Little Crow," Mother Crow said.
"Yes, mother," Little Crow said.
"Listen to me."
"Yes, mother."
"Little Crow," Mother Crow asked, "do you know what's the
most important thing in life?"

Little Crow immediately became very upset. He knew,
because his father and uncles were always telling him, that
crows are clever. Nobody can catch a crow. A crow always
knows a way out — out of anything, even out of difficult
questions. And this was a difficult question. Little Crow sat
down, hunched himself up, put his wings over his ears,
looked at the ground, and opened and closed his beak three
times. Snap, snap, snap.
"Right talking," Little Crow croaked. "We crows talk. But
that's not all we do. We talk right."

RIGHT TALKING

"Yes, yes, yes," Mother Crow said slowly. "RIGHT TALKING.
We know what to say and how to say it."

"We sure do," Little Crow said, and he puffed himself up and
flew off.

He flew until he came to a farm where he saw some pigs in a
pen. He glided down onto a fence post and folded in his wings.

"Hello, friends," Little Crow said to the pigs.

"Hi, buster," said a pig.

"Nice day," said Little Crow.

"Not bad," the pig replied. "But it rained a lot this morning
and it's going to rain again. Makes it sloshy down here.
But we pigs don't mind. We just flop about and make a mess.
Ain't that right guys?"

The pig was eating as he talked, and he sucked and smacked
and slobbered a lot.

"*Must* you talk that way?" Little Crow asked. "You are
splattering all over me you know."

The pig looked at Little Crow with his mouth open and all the other pigs stared.

"Whash? Whash?" the pig asked, and half a wet potato fell out of his mouth.

"You should watch the way you talk," Little Crow said, and he waved his wings at the pig. "Right Talking you know, that's very important. Think before you say something and then say it nicely. I know that because I am a crow, but I want everybody to know — you too."

"Shoo," the pig said.

"No, really," Little Crow said earnestly, and he flew down from the fence post and hopped under a board, for it had indeed begun to rain again, and rain hard. "If you learn how to talk right," Little Crow continued, "you'll be much happier. Here, I'll explain it all to you. You listen to me, you and your friends." But it was raining still harder and the pig looked worried. The water was gushing from the fields, right into the pig pen, and some of the littler pigs were already swimming.

"You see," Little Crow carried on, "if you learn to think before you speak you . . ."

But the pig couldn't hear him anymore, for big raindrops were splashing and spluttering all around them.

"Help, help!" the pig shouted. "We must get out of here! How do we get out of here, Mr. Right Talk?"

"Oh, that's very easy," Little Crow said. "You just fly away. But listen, as I was saying . . ."

The pig was looking around anxiously and trying to swim, and all the other pigs were trying to swim, too. Together they pushed against the fence and the fence broke. So they swam away and climbed onto some dry land. But the board had fallen on Little Crow and he was getting covered with water and he couldn't get any air. He flapped his wings until he could climb onto a piece of fence, and then he passed out.

And that's how his mother found him. She called to his father and together they took him home. He felt very bad. All he wanted to do was sleep, and after a week he still couldn't move about much.

"When will I be all right again, mother?" Little Crow asked. She looked at him and rubbed his head. "Another few days, dear."

"Oh," Little Crow said.

"Don't worry, dear," Mother Crow said. "I'll tell you a story."

Chapter Four

ONCE
upon a time
not so very long ago
Kitten was listening to his mother. He didn't really feel like
listening to her, because he had other things to do, but he was
a reasonably polite little kitten, so he listened.

"Kitten," Mother Cat said.
"Yes, mother," Kitten said.
"Listen to me."
"Yes, mother."
"Kitten," Mother Cat asked, "do you know what's most
important in life?"

Kitten was trying to think of an answer. And while he
thought, he crawled under the couch and rolled over onto his
back. He pulled himself forward by hooking his claws
into the canvas on the bottom of the couch. He was going
quite fast, scooting along on the carpet.
"Kitten!" Mother Cat said sharply, and she narrowed her eyes
and flicked her tail.
"Yes, mother," Kitten said, "I know the answer. What's most
important in life is to do things right. You saw how I moved
along on my back. Wasn't I doing that well?"

"Yes," Mother Cat said, "You were doing fine, and your answer is good too. RIGHT ACTION, that's what it all comes down to. Whatever you do, do it as well as you can."

RIGHT ACTION

His mother closed her eyes and went to sleep, and Kitten went into the garden to see what was going on there. First he met his friend Dog. Kitten rubbed himself against Dog and Dog wagged his tail. Then Kitten saw a ball, a nice red ball. He pounced on it, and then he kicked it and it rolled away. "Ha," said Kitten, and he ran after the ball. He was going to jump on the ball, jump right on top of it. But Dog thought that jumping on a ball was a very nice game, a game for two maybe, and Dog also jumped for the ball. Kitten held the ball between his paws. Dog came running along. "No," Kitten said. He had chased the ball right and jumped the ball right, and so he thought it was his ball. But Dog didn't know that and tried to bite the ball and Kitten hit him on the nose. Scratch! Then Dog, who had nice sharp new teeth, bit Kitten. Mother Cat came running out into the garden. She hissed and yowled and Dog ran away.
But Kitten was bleeding.

Mother Cat picked Kitten up and brought him into the house. She dropped him into his little cane basket and sat next to him, licking his wound. But the wound was deep, and Kitten was in his basket for a long time. After many days Kitten still felt terrible.

"It hurts," Kitten whined. "Will it go on hurting forever, mother?"

"No," Mother Cat said, "it's getting much better, but you have to stay where you are for a bit longer." Kitten looked very sad. Mother Cat felt sorry for him and she purred to comfort him. "Don't worry, Kitten," Mother Cat said. "I'll tell you a story."

Chapter Five

ONCE
upon a time
not so very long ago
Little Squirrel was listening to his mother. He didn't really feel
like listening to her, because he had other things to do,
but he was a reasonably polite little squirrel, so he listened.

"Little Squirrel," Mother Squirrel said.
"Yes, mother," Little Squirrel said.
"Listen to me."
"Yes, mother."
"Little Squirrel," Mother Squirrel asked, "do you know what's
most important in life?"

Little Squirrel curled his long bushy red tail so that its tip
hung above his head.
"Sure," Little Squirrel answered. "What's most important for
us squirrels is that we work and look after ourselves."
Mother Squirrel smiled and patted him between his tufted
ears. "That's right, Little Squirrel," she said, "but that is true
not only for squirrels, but for all animals. All animals have
to support themselves. And do you know what that is called?"
Little Squirrel thought. He thought so hard that his tail
began to tremble.

"It is called . . ." Little Squirrel began. "It is called . . ."

"It is called RIGHT LIVELIHOOD." Mother Squirrel said.

"Right livelihood," repeated Little Squirrel. "That's what it is called."

Little Squirrel rushed off into the forest, and while he rushed he thought. He knew that he was still only a very little squirrel and that his father and mother looked after him and got him all the food he wanted. But he also thought that it might be a wonderful idea if he would help them. Yes, a marvelous idea. So, since he was always very quick about everything, he immediately climbed a tree and looked around for something to pick. The tree was just the right sort of tree — it was full of nuts. "Good," Little Squirrel said, and he began to scurry about, picking all the nuts he could see. As he picked them, he threw them down to the ground. And when there were no more nuts on that branch, he jumped to another branch. He worked and he worked and he picked and he picked. When there wasn't a single nut left on the tree, he slid down and made a nice big heap of all the nuts that he had thrown to the ground.

It was a beautiful heap and he danced around it gleefully. He was so happy that he leaped away and danced around all the trees in the forest.

But it was getting late, and it was also getting dark. Little Squirrel didn't notice. He just danced on and on and shouted with joy and pride at the birds and the other animals.

"I picked the biggest heap of nuts you have ever seen!" shouted Little Squirrel.

But then it became *very* dark, and he couldn't see a thing. He was lost.

And he was cold, too. He climbed onto a branch, and there he crouched and shivered. Every now and then he slept a little, and slowly the night passed. By the time it was light again he had a bad cough. He crawled down off the branch and went to look for his heap of nuts, but he couldn't find it anymore.

When he finally got home, he was very unhappy. "You've been
away all night," his mother said, "and your father and I
have been very worried. What a terrible cough you have!" She
put him in a corner of the nest, covered him up with pine
needles, and gave him some hot milk to drink. Many days
came and went, but he had such a bad cold that he couldn't
stop coughing.

"Mother," Little Squirrel asked, "will this nasty cough
ever go away?"

"Yes," Mother Squirrel answered, "if you stay right here and
keep warm."

Little Squirrel sighed.

"Poor thing," Mother Squirrel said. "You know what? I'll tell
you a story."

Chapter Six

ONCE

upon a time

not so very long ago

Little Rhino was listening to his mother. He didn't really feel

like listening to her, because he had other things to

do, but he was a reasonably polite little rhino, so he listened.

"Little Rhino," Mother Rhino said.

"Yes, mother," Little Rhino said.

"Listen to me."

"Yes, mother."

"Little Rhino," Mother Rhino asked, "do you know what's

most important in life?"

Little Rhino thought. He thought so hard that the folds on the

skin of his forehead crinkled. "RIGHT EFFORT," Little Rhino

said at last, "*that*'s very important."

His mother grunted and tickled him gently with her great

double horn.

RIGHT EFFORT

"Yes," Mother Rhino said, putting her chin on the strong armour plating on Little Rhino's back, "that's the right answer.

Whatever you do must be done with all the power you have. You must never give up. Keep pushing and shoving, and never give in."

Little Rhino trotted off. He felt so good that he began to run. He ran through the fields, and he ran on and on till he came to some bushes. The bushes wanted to stop him, but he grinned and charged straight into them. He couldn't see much, but he didn't care. Twigs snapped and rocks crumbled as he raced on, snorting happily and swaying from side to side. The bush got thicker and thicker, but he only had to use a little more strength as he tunneled through the undergrowth, leaving a long hole behind him.

But a great oak had been waiting for him. When it loomed up in front of Little Rhino, he was going so fast that he couldn't avoid it. The oak was a big thick solid lump of a tree, and it just stood there. His horn hit the oak and went right through its bark, through its soft outer wood, and into the hard inner wood. There it stuck.

WHAM!

And there Little Rhino stood. Little Rhino took a deep breath and smiled. "Push," he said to himself, and he pushed. But nothing happened. He pushed and he pushed some more, and then a tiny little doubt was born in his brain. And it grew and grew.

"Maybe you are stuck," the big doubt said. And the big doubt was right.

And that's how his mother found him, stuck into a tree and crying. His mother called for his father, and together they pulled and pulled. Finally Little Rhino popped free, but he was still crying, for his horn hurt and his head ached dreadfully.

His mother took him home and put him to bed. After a week his headache was almost gone but his horn still hurt.

"Mother," Little Rhino said.

"Yes, dear?"

"How is my horn?"

"It's cracked, dear. It'll be all right again, but you can't go rushing about yet." Little Rhino looked very unhappy. His mother bent down and rubbed his cheek.

"But just to make you feel a little better," Mother Rhino said, "I'll tell you a story."

Chapter Seven

ONCE
upon a time
not so very long ago
Little Rabbit was listening to his mother. He didn't really feel
like listening to her, because he had other things to
do, but he was a reasonably polite little rabbit, so he listened.

"Little Rabbit," Mother Rabbit said.

"Yes, mother," Little Rabbit said.

"Listen to me."

"Yes, mother."

"Little Rabbit," Mother Rabbit scolded, "you are *not* listening
to me. You are jumping about and sniffing and flapping your
ears."

"Sorry, mother," Little Rabbit said.

"Little Rabbit," Mother Rabbit asked, "do you know what's
most important in life?"

"Of course," Little Rabbit answered. "What's most important
in life is to know what's going on around you."

"Right," Mother Rabbit said. "RIGHT AWARENESS, you've
got to know what is happening. You've got to be ready.
Always."

RIGHT AWARENESS

Little Rabbit scampered off, for he wanted to get to the cabbage field. He had been there the day before, but the cabbages weren't ripe yet, so he wanted to see if they were ripe now. On the way he remembered his mother's question and his own good answer, so he stopped and looked about. But looking wasn't enough, so he sniffed, too, and listened very carefully. And he *did* see and smell and hear something. So he dived into a hole — just in time, for the great red fox went by, and he never noticed Little Rabbit. A minute later, the farmer's son appeared with his air gun. Little Rabbit had seen him, too, so the farmer's son never saw Little Rabbit.

The cabbages weren't very tasty yet, but Little Rabbit found six big carrots, and he was just about to start nibbling on a beautifully fresh head of lettuce when he thought he noticed something again. He dropped the lettuce and darted off, but when he looked back, he thought that maybe nothing was there after all. He hopped back and was ready to tear off a crisp leaf when . . . His ears pricked up, his nose trembled, he looked this way and that way. . . No. Just the wind perhaps — the wind moving about in the tall grass. But there *was* a smell, a nasty bitter smell. Fire. Were the fields on fire? He jumped up quickly, trying to look in every direction at once, then he crouched down again. The farmer's son had started a small campfire, that was all. Nothing to worry about.

Once more he started to nibble on the lettuce leaf. But he wasn't quite sure yet. Was everything as it should be? What about the fat green snake his uncles had been telling him about? The fat green snake that slithers through the grass and catches little rabbits. Did he hear the fat green snake? And what about the big black ravens? The ravens who swoop down and grab little rabbits by the neck? He looked up. Did he see the big black ravens? And where was the farmer's son with his gun? And the fox? What had happened to the great red fox? Was he coming back perhaps? He dropped the lettuce leaf and began to run. He ran faster and faster and he ran until he could run no more.

He was wailing when Mother Rabbit found him. He had run for miles and miles, and it took her all day to find him. He couldn't walk. He had run so hard and so much that he had strained all his muscles.

So she had to carry him home.

His legs got a little better every day, but he still couldn't hop properly, and he got very bored.

"Mother," Little Rabbit asked.

"Yes, Little Rabbit?"

"Can't I go out for a bit, mother? Just a few steps maybe?"

"No, Little Rabbit," Mother Rabbit said, "not just yet." Little Rabbit tried very hard not to cry.

"I think I'll tell you a story," Mother Rabbit said.

Chapter Eight

ONCE

upon a time

not so very long ago

Little Sloth was listening to his mother. He didn't really feel
like listening to her, because he had other things to do, but he
was a reasonably polite little sloth, so he listened.

"Little Sloth," Mother Sloth said.

"Yes, mother," Little Sloth said.

"Listen to me."

"Yes, mother."

"Little Sloth," Mother Sloth asked, "do you know what's most
important in life?"

There wasn't any more talk for some time, but finally Little
Sloth shook himself and answered.

"Yes," Little Sloth said.

"What?" Mother Sloth asked.

"RIGHT MEDITATION," Little Sloth said.

RIGHT MEDITATION

"And what's Right Meditation?" Mother Sloth asked.

"To really get down into things," Little Sloth said slowly. "To think so deeply that you know what things really are."

"Right," Mother Sloth said. "To keep very still and to go very deep, that's it."

And that was the beginning of a long silence. Little Sloth liked long silences, and he liked using them. He had been hanging upside down from his branch, and he had been looking at the sky, the great empty blue sky. But right now his mother was hanging above him, and she was in the way. So he began to shift along the branch, very slowly, until finally he only saw the sky. He took a deep breath and dug his twenty nails firmly into the branch.

"Sky," Little Sloth thought. "Great Blue Empty Sky, what are you?"

He thought the same words a hundred times but then he started forgetting words. First he forgot "what are you?" Then he forgot "great" and then "blue" and then "empty."

"Sky," Little Sloth thought, and he breathed even more deeply and slowly. And as he kept thinking "sky," everything else began to stop and disappear. He no longer heard the sounds of the forest, and he no longer knew that he was hanging from a branch, and finally he even forgot that he was Little Sloth. There was nothing but the sky, and the sky was unbelievably beautiful.

His mother, who had been climbing about in the tree to get food and to talk to the other sloths, began to worry.

"Little Sloth," Mother Sloth called. But Little Sloth didn't answer. She shook him, but he still didn't say anything. And Father Sloth, who had been hanging from a branch on the other side of the tree, came down, too, and shook him.

"He has been hanging there for a very long time," Mother Sloth said.

"He should move a little sometimes," Father Sloth said. "Has he eaten?"

"No," Mother Sloth said.

"Let's get him off that branch," Father Sloth said. It was hard work. Little Sloth had dug his nails so deeply into the word that his parents had to pry them loose, one by one. When they were all loose, Mother Sloth and Father Sloth held him and carried him and rubbed his arms and his legs.

Finally Little Sloth opened his eyes. "Where am I?"

"Here," Father Sloth said. "You are right here, and your arms and legs are stiff, and we have been rubbing them for hours. Don't you know that you have to move about and eat sometimes?"

So they made him climb about and eat, but his arms and legs were still stiff.

"Mother," Little Sloth said.

"Yes?"

"I want to hang down from my branch again. Just for a little while."

"No," Mother Sloth said.

"Why not, mother?"

"Because you are not an apple or a pear. Sloths hang from trees, but not all the time."

"Aw, *please*, mother," Little Sloth begged.

"Hush now," Mother Sloth said. "You move about on your branch for a bit, and I'll hang above you and tell you seven stories. We have plenty of time."

And this is what Mother Sloth told Little Sloth:

ONCE
upon a time
not so very long ago
(it could even be now
or, perhaps, tomorrow
or the day after)

Little Owl was listening to his mother. He didn't really feel like
listening to her, because he had other things to do,
but he was a reasonably polite little owl so he listened.

"Little Owl," Mother Owl said.
"Yes, mother," Little Owl said.
"Listen to me."
"Yes, mother."
"Little Owl," Mother Owl asked, "do you know what's most
important in life?"

Little Owl and Little Koala Bear and Little Crow and Kitten
and Little Squirrel and Little Rhino and Little Rabbit and
Little Sloth all got into trouble. And they were all trying to do
the right thing.

So some time later they all met, and when they met they talked a lot and they got on very well together. They came up with a great plan. They thought it might be a very good idea if they all helped each other do the right thing.

So together they went on a long journey.
And together they made it.

Don't ask me what happened at the end.

The end is very far and very few animals
(and humans, too) have been there.

So I don't know.

But I would like to know.

And one day . . . One Day . . .
it may even be right now or
perhaps tomorrow or the day after . . .
you and I and everyone
will find out.